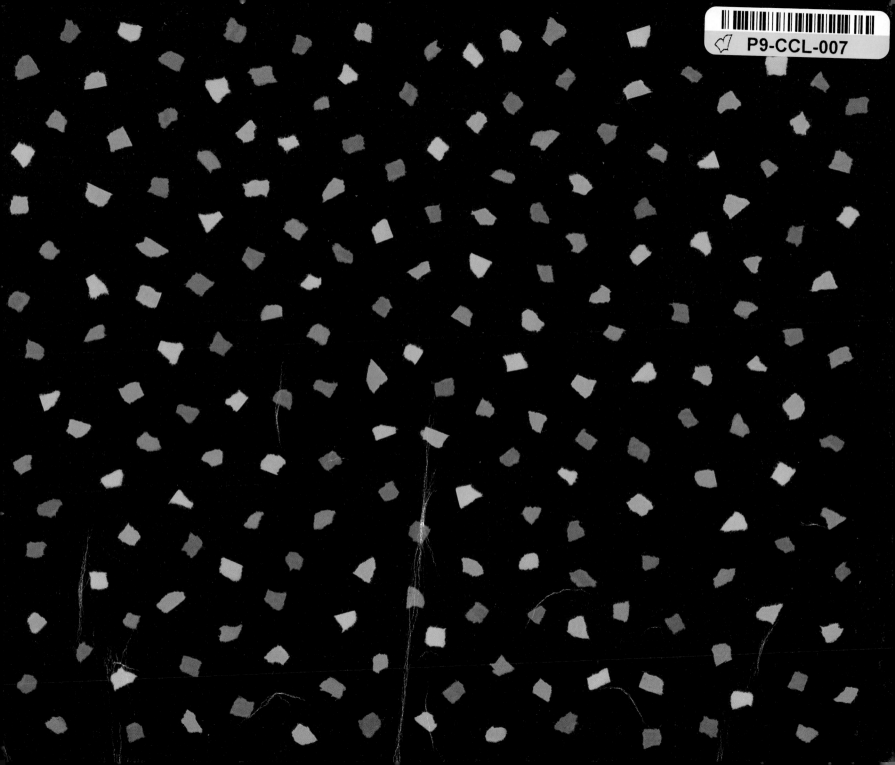

Dedicated to
Peter Newell,
Creator of <u>The Hole Book</u>

THE ARTWORK WAS DONE
USING MIXED MEDIA AND
COLLAGE ON KRAFT PAPER

THERE WAS AN OLD LADY WHO SWALLOWED A FLY

Simms Taback

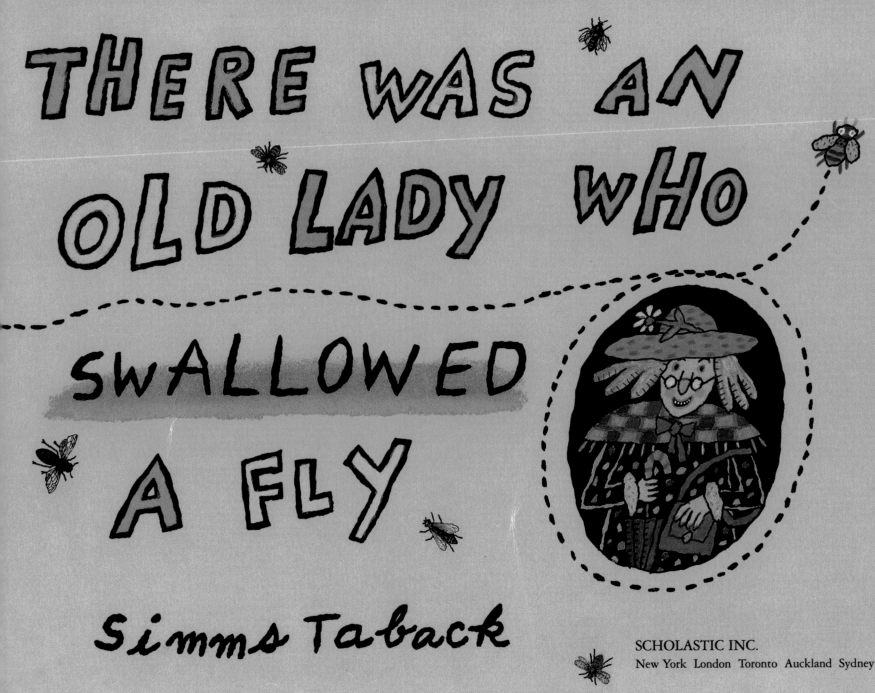

SCHOLASTIC INC.
New York London Toronto Auckland Sydney

There was an old lady who swallowed a fly.

SPIDER'S SOUP

SUPPER RECIPE:
1 FLY, 1 HORNET, 2 WASPS
AND 1/2 CATERPILLAR
SAUTÉ IN WORM JUICE UNTIL
DONE AND SERVE—

That wiggled and jiggled and tickled inside her.

She swallowed the **bird** to catch the spider.

She swallowed the spider to catch the fly.

I don't *know why* she swallowed the fly.

Perhaps she'll die. she'll leave us high and dry.

There was an old lady who swallowed a Cat.

She swallowed the **cat** to catch the **bird**.

She swallowed the **bird** to catch the spider.

she swallowed the **spider** to catch the **fly**.

I don't *know why*

She swallowed **the fly.**

Perhaps she'll **die.** I hope it's a lie

There was an old lady who swallowed a dog.

She went whole hog to swallow the dog.

She swallowed the **dog** to catch the **cat.**

She swallowed the **cat** to catch the **bird.**

She swallowed the **bird** to catch the **spider.**

she swallowed the spider

to catch the **fly.**

I don't

know why

She swallowed the fly.

Perhaps she'll die.

There's a tear in my eye.

was who swallowed a COW.

THERE WAS AN OLD LADY WHO SWALLOWED A FLY, a favorite American folk poem, was first heard in the United States in the 1940's. Several different versions from Georgia, Colorado and Ohio were collected for <u>Hoosier Folklore</u> (Dec. 1947), but its true author remains unknown.